# D-Day!

First published in 1998 by Franklin Watts

This paperback edition published in 1999

Franklin Watts
96 Leonard Street
London EC2A 4XD

Franklin Watts Australia
14 Mars Road
Lane Cove
NSW 2066

**Editor:** Kyla Barber
**Designer:** Jason Anscomb
**Consultant:** Dr Anne Millard, BA Hons, Dip Ed, PhD

A CIP catalogue record for this book
is available from the British Library.

ISBN   0 7496 3446 4 (pbk)
       0 7496 3208 9 (hbk)

Dewey Classification 941.084

Printed in Great Britain

# D-Day!

by
**Dennis Hamley**

**Illustrations George Buchanan**

# W
## FRANKLIN WATTS
### NEW YORK•LONDON•SYDNEY

## 1

## Is Your Journey Really Necessary?

D-Day, the day of the Normandy landings, was on 6th June 1944. The weather was terrible, but that wasn't the only reason Philip was worried. When an announcer on the wireless said that British and American armies had landed Philip shouted out loud,

"It'll be awful. They've got no chance against the Jerries. What will happen to Ira? Everyone was cheering so loudly they took no notice. But Philip couldn't cheer. Because he *knew*.

● ● ● ● ●

Two months before, Philip and his mum were a long way from home. They had visited Aunt Edie in Suffolk – quiet and boring. There was just a cousin called Kathleen, a few months older than Philip, and her tiny brother Brian. Not much chance of a good time with *them*. Mum had come because Aunt Edie's husband, Uncle Jack, was in the RAF. He had been posted away with his squadron. Mum said Aunt Edie needed cheering up. All those Spitfires had flown from their base down the road to somewhere south of London. Not even Jack would tell her where. No wonder she was upset.

"Why wouldn't he say?" Aunt Edie wailed. "I hate the Air Force. Jack got home nearly every day when there wasn't a flap on. Now I don't know when I'll see him." Then she looked at Mum and her voice got quite hard and envious. "You're lucky. Your Jim's not in the services. He just repairs telephones in his own town."

"It's not his fault if he's a skilled man in a reserved occupation," Mum answered. "They don't want everybody fighting. Besides, they trust him in top-secret places." *We'll never cheer Aunt Edie up,* Philip thought. *If she and Mum are going to argue, why did we come?* Anyway, Uncle Jack didn't *fly* Spitfires – Philip would have been impressed if he had. He serviced the engines, which seemed no more exciting than Dad tinkering with the engine of his Post Office van. If you were in the Air Force or Navy or Army, why not do something *heroic*? Like

Ira, the American soldier boyfriend of his elder sister Maisie.

The Easter holidays and windy, showery April were here. News about the war was cheering people up at last. The British and Americans had chased the Germans out of North Africa and Sicily and would soon have them out of Italy as well. In the east, the Russians were pushing the Germans back too. Every night RAF bombers flew over Germany dropping bombs and, every day, American Flying Fortresses did the same. How could Adolf Hitler keep going?

But the trouble was, keep going was what he did. Those Jerries wouldn't lie down. At this rate the war would last for ever. Unless something big happened.

Philip often saw posters saying - SECOND FRONT NOW. There had to be a Second Front one day. At the moment Hitler was using most of his strength in the east, against Russia. Hitler had to be given something big to think about in the west. We had to turn the Germans out of France, Belgium and Holland. We had to go back to France some day and get rid of those terrible memories of Dunkirk, when our  army came home in little boats, defeated, their weapons captured or thrown away.

At least the journey to Aunt Edie's was fun. Though Mum didn't seem to think so. They'd come on a green electric train from their station a few miles north of Portsmouth on the south coast of England, into Waterloo in London. Then underground to Liverpool Street – an echoing cavern with a high roof, choking with smoke, steam and the smell of sulphur. They boarded a train of dirty carriages made of varnished wood, full of servicemen. Mum shrank into a seat by the window, and said, "I wish we hadn't come now."

Philip had seen her looking at the big posters that asked "IS YOUR JOURNEY REALLY NECESSARY?" Not until she'd safely bought the tickets was he sure she wouldn't say "No, it isn't" and drag him back home. But after a couple of days with Aunt Edie, Kathleen and Brian, Philip was sure their journey wasn't really necessary after all.

## 2

## A Bike Ride to Where?

For two days it rained. Kathleen's games
and books were only for girls. Philip found
Ludo and Snakes and Ladders in a
cupboard upstairs. He'd tried to play them
with Kathleen, but they argued and
accused each other of cheating. So he tried

to teach them to Brian, who didn't get the point and had more fun sweeping the counters off the boards.

"Mum," Philip said that night after they'd put up the blackout. "I'm not enjoying this."

"Well, you'll have to stay until I'm good and ready to go." When he looked sulky, she said, "Cheer up, love. The sun will shine tomorrow."

And it did. Suddenly everything outside looked rather good.

"We're going into the village to do some shopping while there are still a few coupons in the ration books," said Aunt Edie. "Brian could do with some fresh air." She and Mum seemed to be getting on better now. "Why don't you two go on a nice long walk?"

Even Aunt Edie couldn't mistake the look of horror on the faces of both Philip and Kathleen. "Or," she said desperately, "you could have a bike ride. I'm sure you could ride Jack's if you let the saddle down, Philip. It's in the shed."

"I bet he can't ride a bike," said Kathleen.

Philip didn't bother to answer.

"Show me where," he said.

Uncle Jack's bike was a big, rickety old thing. Even when Philip had found a spanner and let the saddle right down, his feet only just reached the pedals.

"I knew you couldn't ride it," said Kathleen. Privately Philip agreed, but he wouldn't say so. "I could ride this to Berlin and back," he replied.

He gingerly got on, pushed tentatively on a pedal and swayed dangerously before he found his balance. Then cautiously he set off.

"Told you," he shouted over his shoulder as Kathleen followed. She soon caught up. They rode on silently. Then Philip spoke. "Where to?"

"We could go to the next village."

Because every signpost in the country had been taken down so the Germans wouldn't know where they were if they invaded, Philip had no idea where 'the next village' was. He didn't care either.

"Where's the RAF camp your dad was at?" he asked. Even a deserted airfield would be more interesting than a boring village.

"Ooh," Kathleen said. "We aren't allowed."

"Why not? There's nobody there now."

"Anyway, it's too far."

"How can it be if your dad went on his bike?"

"I'm not going there."

"Then I'll go on my own. If I get lost, you'll have to tell my mum."

Kathleen rode on saying nothing. Then: "All right. It's your fault if we get into trouble." She turned left down a new road made of concrete blocks "This way."

A mile on, they came to a high wire
perimeter fence. Kathleen was nervous.

"Someone might see us," she said.

"How can anybody see us if they've all
gone?" Philip scoffed.

"I won't go any further," said Kathleen.

Philip gave in. Really, now he was close
to the fence, saw padlocked gates, a white
guardroom on the other side and low, sinister
buildings beyond, he too felt, well, a bit
scared. "All right," he said. "Let's leave the
bikes here. We can creep round the fence."

"What for?"

"It's an Air Force camp. There may be things to see."

"But they've gone. You said there'd be nobody here."

"I know. But, well, they might have left something behind."

"I'm going home," said Kathleen.

"Please yourself," Philip answered.

He plunged into the long grass growing outside the fence and crept through it as if he was leading a commando raid. Soon he had forgotten all about Kathleen and the bikes.

## 3

## Finding Something Weird

He continued for what seemed like forever. Sometimes the grass was short. Surely he could be seen for miles. Sometimes he was scratched and stung by brambles and nettles. Sometimes thick bushes grew up against the fence and he had to push his way through like the British soldiers fighting the Japanese in the jungles of Burma. Then he thought, *Sooner or later I've got to get back through that lot.*

By then he'd gone in a great circle to the other side of the airfield, miles from the gates. And now there was a sight before him which made him catch his breath with excitement.

Tanks. Row upon row. Beyond them, lined up on the runway, planes.

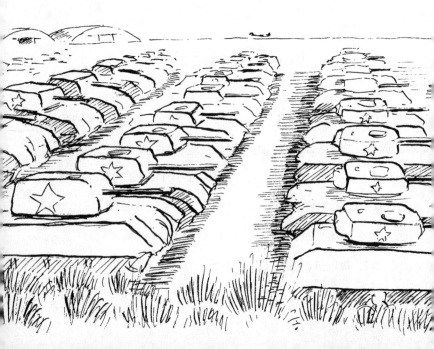

He knew whose tanks were which. These were American. From this distance the dark olive green monsters with one white star painted on the turret looked like Shermans. And the planes. He'd read his aircraft spotter's books. These were Mustangs – single-seat fighters like Spitfires. Line upon line. And P-47s with those strange double fuselages that everybody knew.

There they stood, silent, deserted. Waiting, for the huge engines to roar into

life, the tanks to move away, the planes to take off. Where to? Where else? France.

*"The Second Front,"* he whispered. Oh, how he'd love to get close. Dare he? If only there was a gap in the wire . . .

He pulled at the tough wire mesh. No good. Except – near one concrete post, could he lift the netting enough to squeeze under? He could try. He scrabbled underneath like a dog burying a bone – yes, there was just enough room. Heave, squeeze – he was through.

The nearest tank was fifty yards away. Carefully checking

that nobody was watching, he stole towards it. Halfway there, he stopped.

Something was wrong. This tank was shaking in the wind. And what was so strange about its tracks?

Then he knew – there was no mistake. This was no tank. This was a wooden framework with painted canvas tacked on. Turret, tracks – fake. The huge gun barrel – a long piece of wood.

The next was the same. And the next.

What about the planes? The same. No landing wheels – just sticks on blocks supporting wooden wings which would never take to the air.

Suddenly he wanted to cry. Was this all the great rich American allies could manage – a load of dummies? He turned, ran blindly back to the fence, scrambled under and started the long crawl to the gate.

Kathleen was still with the bikes at the gate. But who was here as well? Two men in uniform – light khaki, in soft material like Ira's. Their brown boots gleamed, their white belts stared, their round steel helmets shone. Most alarmingly, revolvers hung on their belts and they carried menacing sub-machine guns. Their armbands said USMP. Philip knew this must stand for "United States Military Police".

Kathleen was pale and shaking.

"They were in the guard-room," she said. "They saw us."

"You bet we did, miss," said the smaller of the two men.

The other man
was huge. Three
upside-down
stripes were
sewn
on his
arm. A sergeant.
"What are you
two?" he demanded.
"Spies or sump'n?"

"No," Philip
said indignantly,
although his heart
was racing.

"My dad was stationed here," said
Kathleen. "I was showing Philip where."
That was good of her, he thought.

"So he went off on his own, did he?
And saw things he shouldn't?"

"I didn't see anything," Philip

replied. Well, he hadn't. Nothing a spy
would be interested in, anyway. Except –
a terrible thought had entered his mind.

"Are you sure? I don't trust you
English kids."

"Why not?" Philip was angry. "My
sister's going to marry an American
soldier."

"Look, buster, that's what all the
Limey broads say."

"Aw, gee, Chuck," said the other
military policeman. "They're only kids.
Let 'em go."

The sergeant
looked down on
them for a long
time, not
saying a word,
fingering the
trigger on

the sub-machine gun. Philip had visions of army prisons and interrogations.

At last he said. "All right. This time. But don't let us see you here any more."

They got on the bikes and rode off. But before they'd taken three turns of the pedals, a voice roared, "Hey, we want you again."

With hearts like lead they turned. Terrified, they faced the two men. Chuck was feeling in his top pocket. So was his companion. Kathleen and Philip waited.

Then the Americans handed over two packets of chewing gum each. "And don't come back," said Chuck. "Because there ain't no more."

## 4

### Ira's Leaving

Philip and his mum went home the following week. When they got back, they found Maisie very upset.

"Ira's going away with his division. I may never see him again." She flopped down on the sofa and wailed uncontrollably.

"Of course you will, dear," Mum said uselessly. Nobody was going to comfort Maisie now.

"He's not gone yet, though?" said Philip – a hopeful half-question.

"Tomorrow. And he can't say where."

So Maisie was wrong. At least they'd see him tonight. Philip liked Ira. He liked the way he tried to interest him in baseball. He liked how in turn Ira pretended he was interested in the football results and who was top of the League South. And, no, Philip didn't only like Ira because he gave him gum and candy. Though it helped.

"Of course, you know what this means,"

said Dad when he came home from work. "Something big's going to happen."

Really, they all knew that. The town crawled with soldiers and airmen – British, Americans, Australians, Canadians, New Zealanders, South Africans. Polish, Czech and French as well. Convoys of tanks and lorries hauling guns passed through endlessly. And there were sailors up from Portsmouth too. When Dad came back from the pub he often had tales of fights – sailors setting about airmen, American soldiers fighting British infantrymen. Yes, there was tension i the air. What was this great build-up preparing us for?

"Well, of course, I pick up a lot in my job," said Dad with the air of one entrusted with great secrets. He spent most of his time working on a big Air Force base. He was responsible for servicing every telephone and every teleprinter there. "And when I'm in the Operations Room I see top-secret messages coming in," he said proudly. "But it's as

much as my life's worth to tell anybody."

Philip didn't doubt either that he saw the messages or that he wouldn't dare tell. Which was a pity. Because Dad might be able to solve the mystery of the wood and canvas tanks and planes on the airfield in Suffolk.

Not a night had passed without Philip lying awake for hours thinking about it. Why were they there? Everybody said how strong the Yanks were, how they had so many tanks and planes and ships and how we could never win the war without them. But if all their wonderful weapons were just dummies after all? Who were the Americans trying to kid? Us? No, Philip just didn't get it.

That evening, Ira came for supper. This was to be a big night. Mum had baked a cake specially and cracked the entire egg ration for the week into it.

Ira's uniform was newly pressed. His boots shone. His slim figure and face looked, even to Philip, very young for an infantryman who'd already fought in North Africa.

As they ate, there was little talking. It was as if everyone knew this was an evening they would never forget. Whatever happened afterwards, nothing would ever be the same again.

Maisie had met Ira a year before when his division had been sent to a base nearby for training. She had been to a dance and had come home with stories of this wonderful American soldier. After that, she would only listen to music played by Glenn Miller's band and horrified her mother by practising the jitterbug every spare moment.

"When I was your age, we danced properly," Mum would say. But when Maisie brought Ira home for the first time, everyone liked him at once. He was tall, lean and tanned, and spoke with a soft voice which made Philip realise for the first time that the Americans he heard on the wireless were real people.

Soon, Ira visited regularly. Within two months everyone knew he was not like Maisie's other boyfriends.

"Jim," Mum said one night to Dad as Philip

read his comic, "I reckon those two are going to get engaged. I've never seen our Maisie like this."

"Why shouldn't they?" Dad replied. "I like the lad. She could do a lot worse."

"But what if he takes her away to America?"

"They might have a better life than we will after the war," said Dad.

When they had eaten, Ira addressed Dad. "Sir," he said. "We're out of here tomorrow and I have a feeling we won't be back."

There was an indrawn hiss of breath

from everybody. "No," he said quickly.
"We're not going to France yet. We're
being sent for special training. I don't
know what in, but it's going to be hard
and whatever it is it will make us ready for
the great day when it comes."

Nobody said a word. Ira continued.

"So what I want to say is this. I may
not come back because this is a war we're

fighting. But Maisie and I have talked a lot and we're agreed that if I get out of it in one piece we want to get married and live back in the States. I'll give her a good life, be sure about that. But for now I want to go away knowing we have your consent."

He must have seen that Mum was trying very hard to hide her tears at the thought of Maisie leaving them and going to live on the other side of the Atlantic Ocean. But they all knew it would happen and they liked Ira too much to be anything but pleased.

Philip, though, was thinking of something else. Where was Ira going

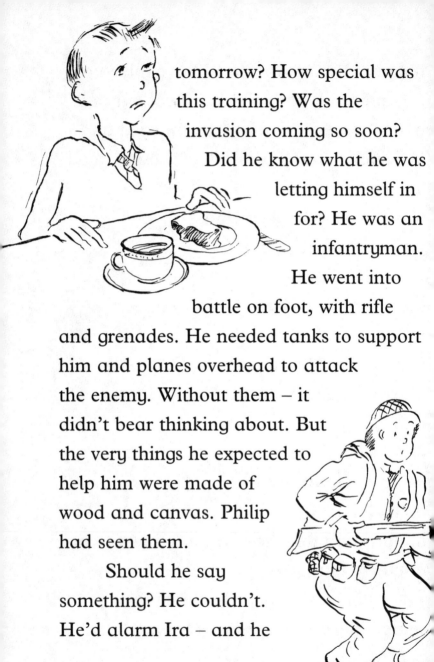

tomorrow? How special was this training? Was the invasion coming so soon? Did he know what he was letting himself in for? He was an infantryman. He went into battle on foot, with rifle and grenades. He needed tanks to support him and planes overhead to attack the enemy. Without them – it didn't bear thinking about. But the very things he expected to help him were made of wood and canvas. Philip had seen them.

Should he say something? He couldn't. He'd alarm Ira – and he

didn't like to think about how upset
Maisie would be. No, he'd have to keep
this awful secret to himself. *Ira wouldn't
be coming back.*

Ira looked at his watch.
"Time for Jack Benny on
the radio," he said.

Everybody
brightened up. They
knew that with Ira
everything stopped for
the Jack Benny Show.
Well, if Maisie was going
to live in America, she'd have
to find out why the Yanks thought
it was funny.

Next day Ira left, but Maisie couldn't
get time off from the parachute factory
where she worked to go to the station and
say a final goodbye. There were a lot of

unhappy girls left behind. When the Americans were gone, a gloom settled over the town. The coming of a new unit to take their place didn't help because somehow everyone knew they wouldn't be there long. But still the tanks and lorries and guns came through and soon the gloom went and everybody was filled with a strange excitement. Something big was near. Winston Churchill, General Eisenhower, General Montgomery – they were cooking something up.

# 5

## Keeping Secrets

May passed. June came. But summer
didn't seem to come with it. The weather
worsened. Grey clouds whipped across the
sky. Rain scudded down. Gales roared,
dislodging tiles and knocking down
chimney pots. On the coast, great waves

burst against the quays of Portsmouth harbour. Huge battleships, fast cruisers, slee destroyers rocked sickeningly at anchor. There'd be no invading done until this lot died down, surely.

Even so, all through May, there was more and more excitement, more listening to the news on the BBC, reading newspapers, studying the maps in them and plotting the direction of the little arrows with Union Jacks, Stars and Stripes, Hammers and Sickles and Swastikas on them. In Italy, Allied soldiers pushed on to Rome: Soviet

troops were driving the Germans out of Russia. Wherever you looked, Hitler was on the run. Surely it could not be long before the great fleet set sail across the channel. Just as soon as these storms died down.

But the nearer the day came, the more Philip's fears grew. He couldn't forget what he'd seen that strange day in Suffolk. Three letters came from Ira addressed to Maisie. She read them until she knew them off by heart. But when they asked her where he was, she replied, "He doesn't say. They've been censored."

One day towards the end of May, Dad came home shaking with excitement. The van screeched to a halt outside the house and he dashed inside. At first he looked as if he wanted to shout out loud. But then he stopped – almost as if he daren't say a word.

"What's the matter, Jim?" asked Mum.

"I've seen it," he said as soon as he was through the door and taken his dripping overcoat off. "I know what's going to happen."

"What are you talking about?" said Mum.

"There was a signal on the teleprinter this morning. Top secret. I read it."

"Then you mustn't tell us," said Mum. "You signed the Official Secrets Act."

"You said it's as much as your life's worth," said Philip.

"Remember the posters. CARELESS TALK COSTS LIVES," said Maisie.

"But I've got to tell *somebody*. I can trust all of you to keep it to yourselves, can't I?"

"You shouldn't do it, Jim," said Mum.

"But I'd never say a word in the pub. I've just got to get it off my chest somehow." They could see he'd burst if he didn't.

"Anyway, it doesn't matter now. It's too late for anyone to do anything about it."

"Well, I wouldn't tell," said Philip.

"Nor me," said Maisie.

"Well, you know I don't gossip," said Mum. That was true, thought Philip. She never shared all her friends' love of a bit of scandal. "Besides," she said. "I don't expect I'll understand a word of it."

"All right, then," said Dad. "Well, I was in the Operations Room this morning. This signal came though on the teleprinter. It wasn't in code even though it was marked TOP SECRET. I could read it easily."

Philip felt excitement welling through him. "Go on, Dad," he said.

"I couldn't believe what it said." By now, Dad was gabbling so much the words could hardly be made out. "All this what's been going on round here – it's just a big trick. The invasion's not from here at all. The main army's in the east, all the way up from the Thames, through Suffolk and Norfolk to the Wash. They're going to land round Calais and up in Norway."

"So what's all the fuss here been?" said Mum. "It seems a waste of time to me."

"To fool the Jerries," said Dad. "It must be. Like it's fooled us."

"Does that mean Ira won't have to go?" said Maisie.

"I reckon they'll have sent him to Norfolk or Suffolk to join the rest," said Dad. "He'll be in the first wave."

Maisie's face turned pale. "Now look what you've done," said Mum.

"You've got to face facts," said Dad. "It's no use fooling yourself."

But Philip said nothing. He was facing a few facts of his own. He'd been right all along. They'd sent Ira off to a place where the tanks were wooden and the planes

canvas. He'd be marching into certain death against an enemy determined to keep him out.

He turned miserably towards Maisie. He should tell his sister. She ought to know the truth.

He drew breath to speak. Then he stopped. Maisie sat on the settee, her face drawn, trying not to cry. How could he say a word? Why make things worse?

Besides, he felt awful. It must be the weather. He had a cold coming on.

Philip couldn't sleep that night. Outside, the storm raged, the gale whined round the house, raindrops whipped against the window. His dreadful knowledge and the oncoming cold meant he couldn't possibly go to school next day.

And that was how he came to be at home in the morning. The storm had died down.

But something else was different. What was it?

He looked out of the window and listened. Nothing. It was strangely quiet.

No army lorries, no guns, no tanks passed through. No planes flew overhead. Where had they gone?

At half past ten he knew, listening to the wireless and "Music While You Work" and hearing the announcement: "Under command of General Eisenhower, Allied naval forces, supported by strong air forces, began landing Allied armies this morning."

Now he could do no more than shout, "It'll be awful. They've got no chance against the Jerries. What will happen to Ira?"

# 6

## And Next . . .

Slowly, the news came through. No, the
Allies hadn't gone to Calais – or Norway.
The landings were in Normandy.

     Philip sat at home nursing his cold
and thinking. So Dad was wrong. But why
would a top-secret signal tell lies?

Philip was wrong as well. The Americans weren't faking it. There were no armies in Norfolk and Suffolk – except a few dummy tanks and planes and some military policemen guarding them. All the real Allied forces were somewhere else.

So what was it all about?

It was long time before Maisie heard anything about Ira. But in the end, she knew

He had landed on a beach code-named 'Omaha' and had a terrible tale to tell – of how, after all their practice in Devon before the invasion, they jumped out of their landing craft in a storm, right into water which came over their heads. Some drowned with all their kit on.

Ira managed to swim, saw his mates drop all round him, survived the struggle up the beach, was pinned down under the

cliffs, then, when defeat seemed certain, the survivors reorganised, pulled themselves together, fought their way out, beat the enemy back and made a secure position to hold until the next soldiers came.

And then he was taken prisoner.

At least Maisie knew he was safe. When the war was over he'd come home.

And he did. In 1946, Maisie set sail for America, a GI bride.

• • • • •

One night soon after D-Day, the truth dawned on Philip like a lightning flash.

*Of course.* It was the signal Dad saw that was the fake. Who'd be trying to find out what signals like that said? Why, German Intelligence, of course.

And who'd be sending spotter planes high overhead taking photographs? Once again, the Germans.

So that was what the dummy planes were for. From the air they would look real.

And one day, everyone would know. It was just that Philip had found out a bit earlier than most.

# D-Day

## After Dunkirk

The British Army had returned defeated from France in 1940 after a rescue operation at Dunkirk, when ordinary people set sail from England in thousands of unarmed small boats to pick up the soldiers. Ever since, the British had longed to go back and drive the occupying Germans out. But they couldn't do it on their own. Europe was occupied by Hitler's forces from the Channel almost to Moscow. If the Americans had not entered the War in 1941, the D-Day landings could never have happened.

## Second Front Now

In both World Wars the Germans made the mistake of trying to fight on two sides at once – in the east and in the west. Hitler thought Britain was finished and that the Americans would never join in, so he spent all his effort on Soviet Russia. Supporters of the Russians put the *Second Front*

*Now* posters up. They wanted the Allies to attack in the west to help Russia.

## The Normandy Landings

When the British and Americans started planning D-Day – so called simply because it would be the day of decision – they soon realised that this would be the biggest invasion operation the world had ever seen. The planning was tremendous. The Americans called their landing beaches Omaha and Utah. The British called theirs Gold, Sword and Juno. On all the beaches there was terrible fighting, and many soldiers were killed. The worst casualties were on Omaha. But somehow they fought through and in the end the first battles in France were won.

## Fooling the Germans

The Allies managed to deceive the Germans about where the landings would be. With fake wireless signals and messages and dummy tanks and aircraft for spotter planes to

see, they made them think there was a huge army waiting in East Anglia to invade further east. If this hadn't worked, the Allies might have been driven back into the sea.

## The Americans in Britain

From 1942, Britain was full of American soldiers and airmen. They brought candy, chewing gum, nylon stockings and a strange slang with them. For example, a "Limey broad" was a British girl. "Broad" was slang from American films and detective stories, "Limey" was an American term for British, just as we called them "Yanks", the Germans "Jerries" and the Russians "Ivans" or "Russkis". The Americans called the British "Limeys" because in the last century British sailors used to drink gallons of lime juice to stop them getting a disease called scurvy.

  When the Americans left, they often didn't go alone. Thousands of British girls crossed the Atlantic as "GI brides". Maisie was just one among many.

# Sparks: Historical Adventures

## ANCIENT GREECE
**The Great Horse of Troy** – The Trojan War
0 7496 3369 7 (hbk)    0 7496 3538 X (pbk)
**The Winner's Wreath** – Ancient Greek Olympics
0 7496 3368 9 (hbk)    0 7496 3555 X (pbk)

## INVADERS AND SETTLERS
**Boudicca Strikes Back** – The Romans in Britain
0 7496 3366 2 (hbk)    0 7496 3546 0 (pbk)
**Viking Raiders** – A Norse Attack
0 7496 3089 2 (hbk)    0 7496 3457 X (pbk)
**Erik's New Home** – A Viking Town
0 7496 3367 0 (hbk)    0 7496 3552 5 (pbk)
**TALES OF THE ROWDY ROMANS**
**The Great Necklace Hunt**
0 7496 2221 0 (hbk)    0 7496 2628 3 (pbk)
**The Lost Legionary**
0 7496 2222 9 (hbk)    0 7496 2629 1 (pbk)
**The Guard Dog Geese**
0 7496 2331 4 (hbk)    0 7496 2630 5 (pbk)
**A Runaway Donkey**
0 7496 2332 2 (hbk)    0 7496 2631 3 (pbk)

## TUDORS AND STUARTS
**Captain Drake's Orders** – The Armada
0 7496 2556 2 (hbk)    0 7496 3121 X (pbk)
**London's Burning** – The Great Fire of London
0 7496 2557 0 (hbk)    0 7496 3122 8 (pbk)
**Mystery at the Globe** – Shakespeare's Theatre
0 7496 3096 5 (hbk)    0 7496 3449 9 (pbk)
**Plague!** – A Tudor Epidemic
0 7496 3365 4 (hbk)    0 7496 3556 8 (pbk)
**Stranger in the Glen** – Rob Roy
0 7496 2586 4 (hbk)    0 7496 3123 6 (pbk)
**A Dream of Danger** – The Massacre of Glencoe
0 7496 2587 2 (hbk)    0 7496 3124 4 (pbk)
**A Queen's Promise** – Mary Queen of Scots
0 7496 2589 9 (hbk)    0 7496 3125 2 (pbk)
**Over the Sea to Skye** – Bonnie Prince Charlie
0 7496 2588 0 (hbk)    0 7496 3126 0 (pbk)
**TALES OF A TUDOR TEARAWAY**
**A Pig Called Henry**
0 7496 2204 4 (hbk)    0 7496 2625 9 (pbk)
**A Horse Called Deathblow**
0 7496 2205 9 (hbk)    0 7496 2624 0 (pbk)
**Dancing for Captain Drake**
0 7496 2234 2 (hbk)    0 7496 2626 7 (pbk)
**Birthdays are a Serious Business**
0 7496 2235 0 (hbk)    0 7496 2627 5 (pbk)

## VICTORIAN ERA
**The Runaway Slave** – The British Slave Trade
0 7496 3093 0 (hbk)    0 7496 3456 1 (pbk)
**The Sewer Sleuth** – Victorian Cholera
0 7496 2590 2 (hbk)    0 7496 3128 7 (pbk)
**Convict!** – Criminals Sent to Australia
0 7496 2591 0 (hbk)    0 7496 3129 5 (pbk)
**An Indian Adventure** – Victorian India
0 7496 3090 6 (hbk)    0 7496 3451 0 (pbk)
**Farewell to Ireland** – Emigration to America
0 7496 3094 9 (hbk)    0 7496 3448 0 (pbk)

**The Great Hunger** – Famine in Ireland
0 7496 3095 7 (hbk)    0 7496 3447 2 (pbk)
**Fire Down the Pit** – A Welsh Mining Disaster
0 7496 3091 4 (hbk)    0 7496 3450 2 (pbk)
**Tunnel Rescue** – The Great Western Railway
0 7496 3353 0 (hbk)    0 7496 3537 1 (pbk)
**Kidnap on the Canal** – Victorian Waterways
0 7496 3352 2 (hbk)    0 7496 3540 1 (pbk)
**Dr. Barnardo's Boys** – Victorian Charity
0 7496 3358 1 (hbk)    0 7496 3541 X (pbk)
**The Iron Ship** – Brunel's Great Britain
0 7496 3355 7 (hbk)    0 7496 3543 6 (pbk)
**Bodies for Sale** – Victorian Tomb-Robbers
0 7496 3364 6 (hbk)    0 7496 3539 8 (pbk)
**Penny Post Boy** – The Victorian Postal Service
0 7496 3362 X (hbk)    0 7496 3544 4 (pbk)
**The Canal Diggers** – The Manchester Ship Canal
0 7496 3356 5 (hbk)    0 7496 3545 2 (pbk)
**The Tay Bridge Tragedy** – A Victorian Disaster
0 7496 3354 9 (hbk)    0 7496 3547 9 (pbk)
**Stop, Thief!** – The Victorian Police
0 7496 3359 X (hbk)    0 7496 3548 7 (pbk)
**Miss Buss and Miss Beale** – Victorian Schools
0 7496 3360 3 (hbk)    0 7496 3549 5 (pbk)
**Chimney Charlie** – Victorian Chimney Sweeps
0 7496 3351 4 (hbk)    0 7496 3551 7 (pbk)
**Down the Drain** – Victorian Sewers
0 7496 3357 3 (hbk)    0 7496 3550 9 (pbk)
**The Ideal Home** – A Victorian New Town
0 7496 3361 1 (hbk)    0 7496 3553 3 (pbk)
**Stage Struck** – Victorian Music Hall
0 7496 3363 8 (hbk)    0 7496 3554 1 (pbk)
**TRAVELS OF A YOUNG VICTORIAN**
**The Golden Key**
0 7496 2360 8 (hbk)    0 7496 2632 1 (pbk)
**Poppy's Big Push**
0 7496 2361 6 (hbk)    0 7496 2633 X (pbk)
**Poppy's Secret**
0 7496 2374 8 (hbk)    0 7496 2634 8 (pbk)
**The Lost Treasure**
0 7496 2375 6 (hbk)    0 7496 2635 6 (pbk)

## 20th-CENTURY HISTORY
**Fight for the Vote** – The Suffragettes
0 7496 3092 2 (hbk)    0 7496 3452 9 (pbk)
**The Road to London** – The Jarrow March
0 7496 2609 7 (hbk)    0 7496 3132 5 (pbk)
**The Sandbag Secret** – The Blitz
0 7496 2608 9 (hbk)    0 7496 3133 3 (pbk)
**Sid's War** – Evacuation
0 7496 3209 7 (hbk)    0 7496 3445 6 (pbk)
**D-Day!** – Wartime Adventure
0 7496 3208 9 (hbk)    0 7496 3446 4 (pbk)
**The Prisoner** – A Prisoner of War
0 7496 3212 7 (hbk)    0 7496 3455 3 (pbk)
**Escape from Germany** – Wartime Refugees
0 7496 3211 9 (hbk)    0 7496 3454 5 (pbk)
**Flying Bombs** – Wartime Bomb Disposal
0 7496 3210 0 (hbk)    0 7496 3453 7 (pbk)
**12,000 Miles From Home** – Sent to Australia
0 7496 3370 0 (hbk)    0 7496 3542 8 (pbk)